Duncan Cillan

The adventures of Monkey and Bean

'Dinosaur Footprints'

www.monkeyandbean.com

www.woodtoinspire.com

For my wife

The sun came up over Monkey and Bean who eat their breakfast sitting by the lake.

Monkey hurried to eat his bananas while Bean's cheeks swelled from all the peanuts he was eating.

"Look at the beautiful sunshine rising on the lake." Monkey suggested to Bean.

"Hurry Monkey, or we will be late for the tour guide." commented Bean.

"I have almost finished eating my bananas, Bean. I will save these other ones for later." replied Monkey.

"Today will be a very exciting day," explained Ranger Frankie. "We are going to walk to a special place where dinosaurs used to roam. Please now all follow me and if you have any questions just ask."

As the tour led by Ranger Frankie started, nearby mountains, the forest, lakes and rivers began to sing. The sounds of water flowing along mountain streams was all around them and the heavy crack of ice breaking from a nearby glacier seemed to shake the whole world. Wind gently whistled through the trees and stones crunched under the feet of Monkey and Bean as they went in search of dinosaurs.

The tour began their hike into the mountains.

"Wow, look at those footprints, Monkey" suggested Bean. "They are huge. Do you think that they could belong to a dinosaur?"

"Let us explore some more and we will find out," said Monkey. "If we slip away from the Ranger, we can follow the footprints to see where they lead. I will drop some banana skins along the way so we can follow them home again."

The warmth of the afternoon sun had brought everything to life, warming the nearby stream in which Monkey, and Bean paddled their feet.

The trees that surrounded them swayed gently, back and forth, to the rhythm of a gentle breeze. The scent of the trees was all around them. It made the two friends feel like they were in another world with only the sounds of the flowing stream and the rustle of leaves for company.

Monkey and Bean felt as if they had the whole forest to themselves.

But did they?

"I really thought that we would find a dinosaur" said Monkey to Bean. "Do not be too disappointed." replied Bean. "We have still had fun and seen lots of beautiful mountains and trees."

"Wait said Monkey, look over there".

A pair of big friendly eyes was looking at Monkey and Bean through the trees.

Page 7

A pair of big friendly eyes was looking at Monkey and Bean through the trees.

The two friends approached the pair of eyes they could see.

At that moment, the ground shook and the trees parted, some snapping due to the size of the creature before them.

There in front of them was a dinosaur.

"Hello" said the two friends. "I am Monkey and this is my friend Bean. Have you been hiding there for long?"

"Hi there," replied the dinosaur. "I have not been waiting here long, but I am lost. I have not been in this area before and cannot seem to find my way home. My name is Dinosaur by the way."

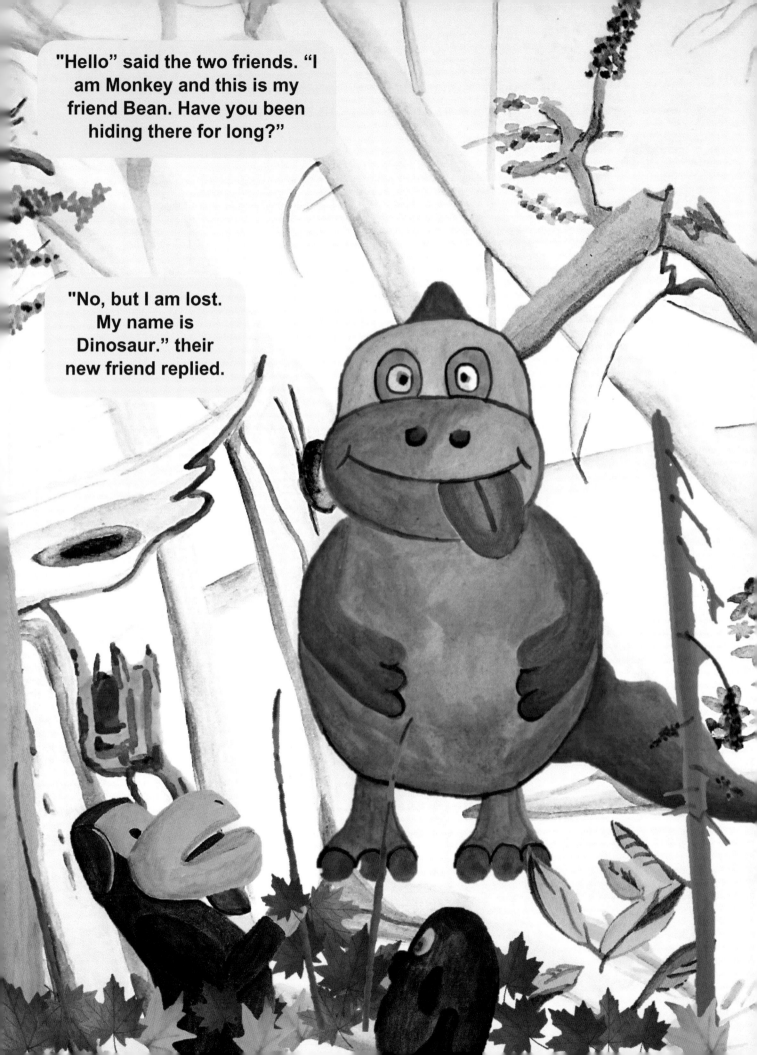

"Why not let us help you" replied Monkey. "Bean is a great map reader. Are you hungry? We have some food that we can share with you."

"That is very kind of you." replied Dinosaur. "Thank you for trying to help me."

The three friends sat on a nearby boulder eating a supper of bananas, peanuts and leaves.

Meanwhile the sun began to set on their day of adventure, exploration and fun.

"Let us try and get you home." said Bean.

"Would you like to sit on my back?" asked Dinosaur. "We can travel a great distance very quickly."

The three friends finished their food and started to make their way in the direction of what they thought might be Dinosaur's home.

In time they came to a big lake. It was so wide the trees on the other side of the lake looked like sticks.

"We have to keep going," said Monkey. "We can climb that mountain on the other side of this lake and get a view from the top."

Page 13

The three friends travelled for many hours until it was dark.

"Look at those strange lights in the sky," said Bean. "You can clearly see that gap in the mountains and the lake."

"That is it," said Dinosaur. "That is where I live."

"We must hurry," said Bean "before the lights disappear and we can no longer find our way."

"I knew we would find the way." said Monkey.

Monkey, Bean and Dinosaur rushed in the direction of the lake. Bright lights lit up the whole sky in magical green and purple colours without which they would not be able to see where they were going.

Page 15

The three friends walked in the direction of the lights they had seen in the sky until they reached Dinosaur's home. It was very dark, and the three friends were quite tired.

"Welcome to my home," said Dinosaur. Us dinosaurs have lived here in this meadow in secret for many years.

"We should go to sleep," suggested Monkey. "It is late".

"Good night Monkey, good night Bean."

"Sleep well Dinosaur." replied our two explorers.

The three friends laid down in the meadow and quickly went to sleep. They were tired by youth and having travelled many miles.

As they slept in the long, tall grass, the stars in the sky shone down uniting them under a blanket of soft sparkling light.

Page 17

The three friends woke up feeling well rested and excited by the day ahead of them. The sun was already shining.

"I know that you will need to get back home soon, but first let me show you this cave."

Led by Dinosaur our three explorers made their way into the cave. First, they had to walk past a huge boulder and underneath a waterfall. The boulder was so large it had trees growing on it, so large that it could only exist in the land of dinosaurs.

"Wow…. This cave is huge." said Monkey.

Monkey and Bean followed Dinosaur into the cave. Though it was dark inside, all around them there were stars shining. Except that they were not stars but diamonds, rubies, sapphires and precious stones.

"I want to thank you for helping me," said Dinosaur. "Will you accept this gift?"

Monkey and Bean looked on in wonder at the giant ruby Dinosaur was holding.

"If you look closely and hold it up to the light," said Dinosaur "and truly believe, you will see me and the other dinosaurs waiting for you next time you visit. With this ruby we will always be together. See how it glows in the dark, like the lights that guided us last night."

"Thank you so much," Monkey and Bean replied. Wow, it is amazing; we will treasure it forever as a memory of our time in this wonderful place."

"If you return the way we came," said Dinosaur, "it will take you to the other side of the mountain. And remember that you will always be welcome here."

The friends parted promising to stay in touch.

Monkey and Bean said goodbye and started to make their way home. Soon they came to a cliff face which they needed to climb down to reach home.

"It looks like a difficult climb." mentioned Bean.

"Do not worry Bean. We will float down to the ground using this giant maple leaf."

When Monkey and Bean got to the ground, they walked back home. This was a huge castle-like building which towered over the landscape. Even the mountains looked small when compared with it.

To their surprise Ranger Frankie was waiting for them. "You must never tell anyone about where you have been," said the Ranger. "The location of the dinosaurs must remain a secret. The valley where they live is rich with rubies and lots of people will flock there to steal them. This will destroy the world of the dinosaurs and they will have nowhere to live."

"You noticed that we had left the group," said Monkey.

"I did, but I knew you would be ok. Thank you for looking after the dinosaur. You were lucky to see it; like everything in life worth knowing, dinosaurs only reveal themselves to those that are worthy and truly kind."

The End

Monkey and Bean will return in

'The Lost Dinosaur Egg'

Featuring 'Turd Bird'

Count and write the number game

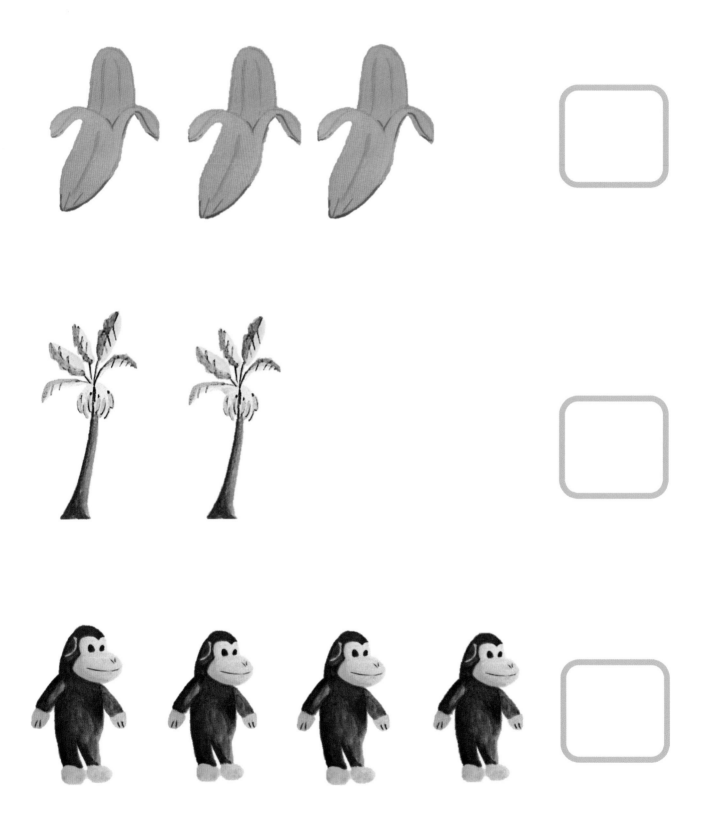

Locations pictured in the book

Castle Mountain (Front Cover)

Consolation Lake Trail

Emerald Lake

Fairmont Banff Springs Hotel

Johnson Canyon Secret Cave

Yoho Lake Pass

Lake Agnes

Lake Louise

Monkey and Bean in 'Dinosaur Footprints' is the second in a series of illustrated children's books by Duncan Gillan. The first book in the series, 'Monkey and Bean journey to Red Island' was published in 2020.

Duncan Gillan is a Cabinet Maker based in London.

"My journey into writing and illustrating children's books provides an opportunity to explore a different medium of art and self-expression. It allows me to relive past adventures and throw in an imaginative twist."

Published to wide praise in 2020 Duncan's first book has proved hugely popular. "I am sincerely grateful to all who purchased my first book. With the publishing of 'Dinosaur Footprints', it's great to see my two favourite characters back exploring and enjoying the world."

The book features 14 full colour hand drawn and painted illustrations, and a fun educational question to support learning.

Monkey and Bean will return in

'The Lost Dinosaur Egg'

www.monkeyandbean.com

www.woodtoinspire.com

Printed in Great Britain
by Amazon